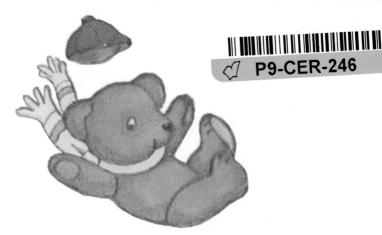

A NOTE TO PARENTS

When your children are ready to "step into reading," giving them the right books—and lots of them—is as crucial as giving them the right food to eat. **Step into Reading Books** present exciting stories and information reinforced with lively, colorful illustrations that make learning to read fun, satisfying, and worthwhile. They are priced so that acquiring an entire library of them is affordable. And they are beginning readers with an important difference—they're written on four levels.

Step 1 Books, with their very large type and extremely simple vocabulary, have been created for the very youngest readers. **Step 2 Books** are both longer and slightly more difficult. **Step 3 Books,** written to mid-second-grade reading levels, are for the child who has acquired even greater reading skills. **Step 4 Books** offer exciting nonfiction for the increasingly proficient reader.

Children develop at different ages. **Step into Reading Books,** with their four levels of reading, are designed to help children become good—and interested—readers *faster*. The grade levels assigned to the four steps—preschool through grade 1 for Step 1, grades 1 through 3 for Step 2, grades 2 and 3 for Step 3, and grades 2 through 4 for Step 4—are intended only as guides. Some children move through all four steps very rapidly; others climb the steps over a period of several years. These books will help your child "step into reading" in style!

Library of Congress Cataloging-in-Publication Data: Phillips, Joan. Lucky bear. (Step into reading. A Step 1 book) SUMMARY: A teddy bear's luck saves him from one calamity after another and eventually finds him a home. [1. Teddy bears—Fiction. 2. Toys—Fiction] I. Miller, J.P., ill. II. Title. III. Series. PZ8.9.P543Lu 1986 [E] 85-14467 ISBN: 0-394-87987-2 (trade); 0-394-97987-7 (lib. bdg.)

Manufactured in the United States of America   23   24   25   26   27   28   29   30

STEP INTO READING is a trademark of Random House, Inc.

Step into Reading

LUCKY BEAR

by Joan Phillips
illustrated by J. P. Miller

A Step 1 Book

Random House 🏠 New York

What a nice bear

I have made.

I like your red hat.

Here is a blue scarf
for you.
Now all you need is a name.

I will name you Lucky.

Here is a good place
for you.

Hello.

I am Lucky.

Let's go out and play.

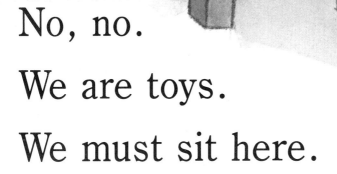

No, no.

We are toys.

We must sit here.

I do not want to sit.

Look!

The window is open.

Lucky me!

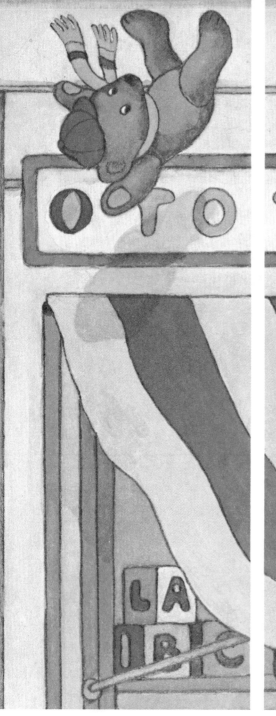

Help!

I am falling!

Oh no!

Here I go!

Good!

I am safe.

Lucky me.

Here is a boat.

Oh no!

It is sinking.

I like water.

But I can not swim.

I am lucky.

Here is a balloon.

Look!

I am flying.

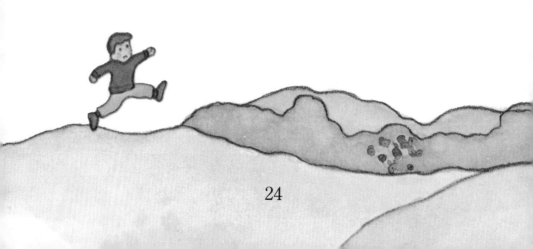

Oh no!
Now I am up
in a tree.

I am lucky.
Here comes
someone to help.

Hi.

I am Ben.

I need a bear.

Hi.

I am Lucky.

I need a boy.

We are both so lucky.